MY CHRISTMAS CRAFT BOOK

MY CHRISTMAS CRAFT BOOK

For Kids

Anna Murray   Lynda Watts

WESTERN®

Western Publishing Company, Inc.
Racine, Wisconsin 53404

CREDITS

Managing editor: Veronica Ross
Art director: Rachael Stone
Photographer: Jonathan Pollock
Assistant photographer: Peter Cassidy
Additional designs by: Cheryl Owen
Editor: Coral Walker
Designer: Cherry Randell
Illustrator: John Hutchinson
Character illustrator: Jo Gapper
Diagram artist: Malcolm Porter
Typeset by: Ian Palmer
Color separation by: Regent Publishing
Services Ltd., Hong Kong

CONTENTS

INTRODUCTION

The weeks leading up to Christmas are some of the most exciting of the year, with so much to plan and prepare. In *My Christmas Craft Book* we show you how to make almost everything you will need to make your Christmas really special. There are lots of decorations to make, and we also show you how to make tempting goodies to eat and a range of fun ideas to give as presents.

Get everything ready before you start, and don't forget to clean up afterward!

BEFORE YOU BEGIN
- Check with an adult before you begin any project.
- Read the instructions first.
- Gather together all the items you need before you begin.
- When using glue or paints, cover your work surface with newspaper or an old cloth.
- Protect your clothes with an apron or wear very old clothes.

WHEN YOU HAVE FINISHED
- Wash paintbrushes and remember to put the tops back on pens, paints, and glue containers.
- Put everything away. Store special pens, paints, glue, and so forth, in plastic containers or cookie tins.
- If you are baking, put away all the ingredients, wash any dishes, and leave the kitchen tidy.

SAFETY FIRST!
You will be able to make most of the projects yourself, but sometimes you will need help. Look out for the SAFETY TIP. It appears on those projects where you will need to ask an adult for help. Remember to use your common sense when using anything hot or sharp, and if in any doubt, ask an adult for advice.

PLEASE REMEMBER THE BASIC RULES OF SAFETY
- Never leave scissors open or lying around where smaller children can reach them.
- Always stick needles and pins into a pincushion or a scrap of cloth when you are not using them.
- Never use an oven or a sharp knife without the help or supervision of an adult.

EQUIPMENT AND INGREDIENTS

Every project will list all the things you need. Many designs use glitter, shiny paper, or tinsel; look among last year's Christmas decorations before buying new materials. The recipes for fudge and gingerbread men require baking ingredients. You will probably find most of the ingredients you need in the kitchen cupboard, but check with an adult before taking anything.

USING PATTERNS

At the back of the book, you will find the patterns you will need to make some of the projects in the book. Using a pencil, trace the pattern you need onto tracing paper. If you are making a project with fabric, cut the pattern out and pin it onto the fabric. Cut out the shape. If you want to cut the pattern out of poster board or construction paper, turn your tracing over, lay it on the back of the poster board or construction paper, and rub firmly over the pattern outline with a pencil. The pattern will transfer onto the firm paper. Cut out this shape.

Once you have gained confidence making some of the projects in this book, go on to adapt the ideas to create some of your own designs.

ADULTS TAKE NOTE

Every project in *My Christmas Craft Book* has been designed with simplicity yet effectiveness in mind. However, some potentially dangerous items such as an oven or a sharp knife are used for some projects. Your involvement will depend on the ability of the child, but we do recommend that you read through any project before it is undertaken.

FELT TREE ORNAMENTS

Leftover braid and scraps of felt can be used to make these cheerful ornaments. Use the shapes shown here or invent your own to suit the materials you have on hand. Snowmen, bells, small Christmas trees, or Santa hats are just a few of the other ideas you might try.

YOU WILL NEED
Tracing paper; pencil
Poster board
Scissors
Fabric glue
Felt in different colors
Assortment of braid,
  ribbons, cord, sequins,
  and lace
Glitter

1 Using a pencil, trace either the boot or the candle pattern on page 54. Turn the tracing over and lay it on the poster board. Rub firmly over the outline with a pencil. The pattern will appear on the poster board. Cut out the shape.

2 To make the boot, coat a large piece of poster board with glue and stick some felt on it. Position the boot pattern on the felt and draw around it. Cut out one boot, then flip the pattern over to cut out a second boot. Glue trims and sequins in a pattern onto the felt side of one boot.

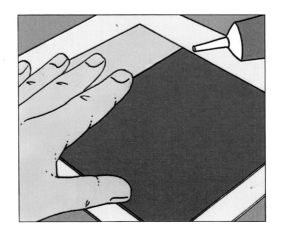

3 Turn the boot over and glue a loop of ribbon or cord to the top. Coat the poster board with glue and stick the plain felt boot to the decorated one.

4 To make the candle, glue a strip of felt at least 5 inches wide onto the poster board. For the flame, cut a strip of yellow felt at least 1½ inches wide and glue to the poster board so that it touches the edge of the candle felt.

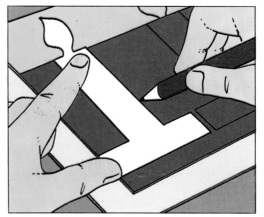

5 Cut out the candle pattern, following the instructions in Step 1. Position the pattern on the felt, as shown, so that the flame is on the yellow felt. Draw around the pattern and cut out. Flip the pattern over to cut out a second candle. Decorate and finish off, following the instructions in Step 3. Sprinkle the flame with glitter to finish.

POP-UP SANTA

Cards that have a pop-up section are expensive to buy, but not that hard to make. Try making several cards, so that you can give one to each friend. Make sure you use construction paper that is firm, not floppy.

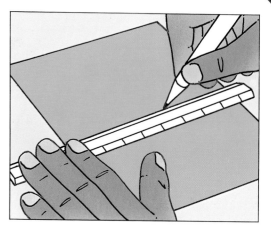

1 On the blue poster board, draw a rectangle 11 inches by 7 inches. Draw a line down the center to divide it in two. Cut out the card and fold it in half.

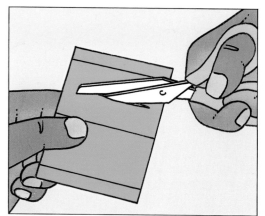

2 Trace the patterns on page 55. Turn the tracings over and lay the body pattern on red paper, the beard on white paper, the sack on brown paper, and the chimney on green. Rub over the outlines with a pencil. The images will appear on the construction paper. Cut out the patterns and the slot in the chimney.

5 Fold the chimney into shape, as shown, and slip the Santa into the slot. Fold a little of Santa's body down and stick it to the inside of the chimney.

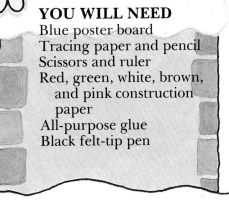

YOU WILL NEED
Blue poster board
Tracing paper and pencil
Scissors and ruler
Red, green, white, brown,
  and pink construction
  paper
All-purpose glue
Black felt-tip pen

6 Position the chimney and Santa inside the card, as shown. This is how it will look when the card is open. Dab glue on the chimney tabs, then stick it in place.

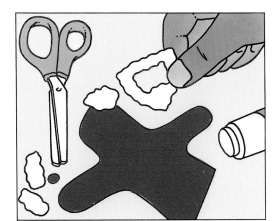

3 Using the body pattern as a guide, cut 2 cuffs and a pompom from white paper and a face from pink paper. Glue all the shapes on the body shape. Draw on the eyes with the black felt-tip pen and add a red nose cut from construction paper.

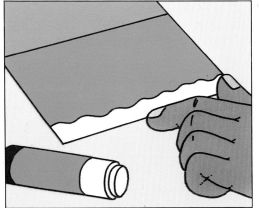

4 To make the roof, draw a rectangle 5½ inches by 7 inches on green paper and cut it out. Stick it to one half of the inside of the card. Cut some extra white paper to look like snow, and glue one piece to the front of the chimney and one to the edge of the green roof.

CHRISTMAS STOCKING

This Christmas, make a special stocking to put beside the fire or to use as a novelty bag for small presents. Use a glue stick for this project, as any of the wetter glues may make the crepe paper's color run.

YOU WILL NEED
Tracing paper and pencil
Scissors and pins
Double-sided crepe paper
Thick sewing thread and
   needle
Scraps of white, black, and
   colored construction
   paper
Glue stick and pen

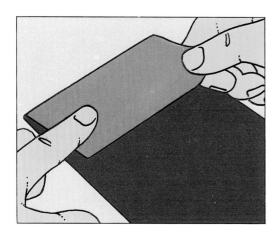

1 Using a pencil, trace the stocking pattern on page 56. Cut out the pattern and pin to a piece of crepe paper that has been folded in half. Carefully cut around the pattern to give 2 stocking shapes. Fold down the top of each stocking to show the second color of crepe paper.

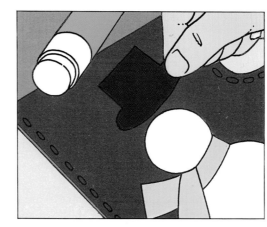

3 Cut a snowman shape from white paper and stick it in place on the stocking. Cut a hat from black paper and a scarf from a different color. Glue them on the snowman.

2 Pin the stockings together and, using the needle and thread, sew around the outer edge, as shown above.

4 Cut a small carrot shape for the nose and circles for buttons and glue them on. Trim the hat with some holly leaves cut from green paper and berries from red. Draw dots for the eyes with the pen.

POTPOURRI SACHETS

These little sachets, filled with perfumed potpourri, make wonderful gifts. You can also hang them from the Christmas tree to give the room a beautiful smell. Look for special Christmas potpourri that smells of oranges, pine, and cinnamon.

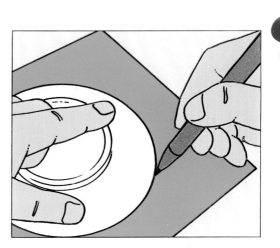

1 Lay out the fabric, wrong side facing you. Place the plate on the fabric and draw around it with the pen. Using the pinking shears, cut out the circle, just inside the pen line.

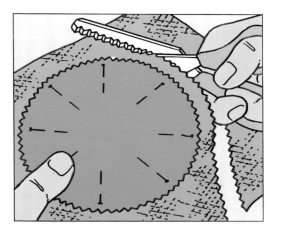

2 Pin the fabric circle to 2 pieces of net. Using pinking shears, cut out 2 slightly larger net circles. Remove the pins. Lay the fabric circle down, wrong side facing you. Place the 2 net circles on top.

14

3 Pour a small mound of potpourri into the center of the circles. Gather the circles up around the potpourri and tightly wrap a rubber band around the fabric. Frill the fabric out at the top.

4 Decorate the sachets with a ribbon bow. Add other trims, such as wired beads, poking the ends of the wire around behind the ribbon. You could stitch or glue a few sequins to the bow as well.

YOU WILL NEED
Printed cotton fabric
Pen and a small plate
Pinking shears; pins
Colored net
Potpourri
Rubber bands
Ribbons
Wired ornaments
  and sequins

RAFFIA WREATH

One of the friendliest Christmas traditions is to hang a festive wreath on the front door. Not only does it cheer up passersby, but it gives a very warm welcome to family and friends.

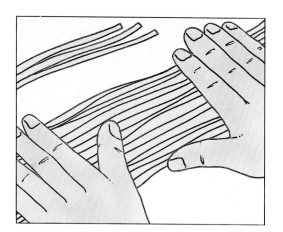

1 Lay the raffia on some paper and smooth it out, as shown. Put a few single lengths of raffia to one side to use as ties. Tie the raffia into a bunch at one end.

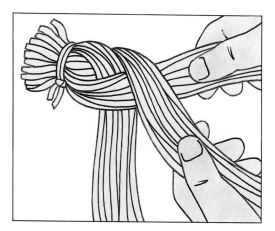

2 Divide the raffia into 3 bundles and braid it as you would hair, taking the outer bunches over the center one. When the braid is complete, tie it firmly at one end with one of the extra pieces of raffia. Trim both ends of the braid.

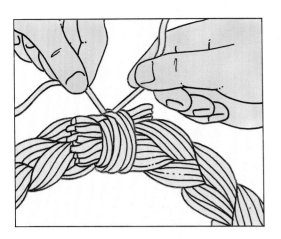

3 Curve the braid into a circle and overlap the ends. Tie them together with raffia, wrapping it around and around the join to completely cover it. Make a firm knot and trim the ends.

4 Cut an 8-inch length of wide ribbon and wrap it over the join, stitching it at the back. Cut another piece of the ribbon about 12 inches long, fold it into a loop, and stitch it to the back of the wreath. Tie the remaining ribbon into a bow and stitch it to the front.

5 Prepare the wired decorations. To wire pinecones, cut a short length of wire and wrap it around the base of the cone, twisting the ends together. Wire cinnamon sticks into small bunches and hide the wire with a ribbon tie. Store-bought trims should have wires already attached.

YOU WILL NEED
Raffia
1 yard of wide ribbon
Needle and thread; scissors
Pinecones
Florist's or fuse wire
Cinnamon sticks
Narrow ribbons
Extra trims like wired berries and leaves (sold at Christmastime)
Gold acrylic paint; paintbrush

6 Press the ends of the wired decorations through to the back of the wreath and twist them into the braid to secure them. When the decoration is complete, paint the wreath with dabs of gold paint.

SAFETY TIP: *Ask an adult to help you prepare the wired decorations.*

FESTIVE FRIDGE MAGNETS

These merry Christmas refrigerator magnets will cheer up anyone working hard in the kitchen during the festive season. They are great fun to make using colored modeling clay that is baked in the oven.

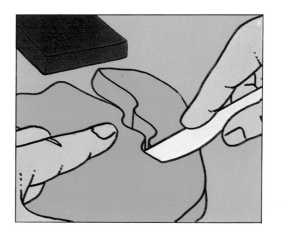

1 Roll out some green and red clay, about ¼ inch thick. Using a blunt knife, cut out some tree shapes from the green clay and cut squares from the red clay.

2 To decorate the tree, roll out yellow clay and cut out a star shape. To make the ornaments, roll pieces of red clay between your finger and thumb. Press them onto the tree. For the presents, roll out some blue clay and cut out strips for the ribbons and bows. Press onto the presents.

3 Bake the clay shapes in an oven, following the instructions on the packet. Wearing oven mitts, remove the shapes from the oven. Leave to cool and harden.

4 Glue a small magnet to the back of each shape. Let the glue dry before using.

YOU WILL NEED
Modeling clay that will harden in the oven
Rolling pin
Blunt knife
Baking sheet
Oven mitts
All-purpose glue
Refrigerator magnets

SAFETY TIP: *Make sure an adult helps you when using the oven.*

FLYING ANGELS

Hang this cute mobile in a doorway or the corner of a room. If you don't want to make a complete mobile, the individual angels can be used as Christmas tree ornaments.

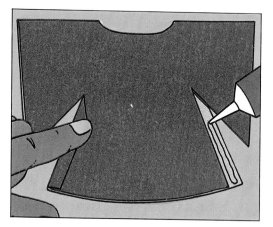

1 Using a pencil, trace the dress pattern on page 57. Cut out the pattern and pin to the crepe paper. Cut out the dress, then fold it in half along the fold line and cut away the neck hole. Fold the tabs back and glue them down. Glue the edges of the sleeves together.

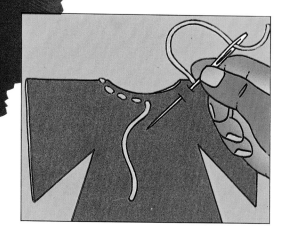

2 Thread the needle with gold yarn. Sew around the neck opening, leaving long ends of yarn.

20

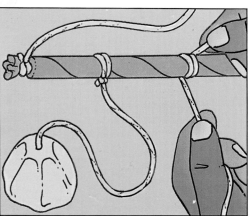

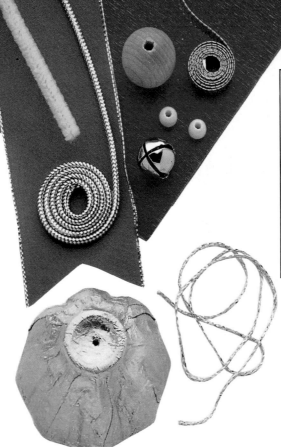

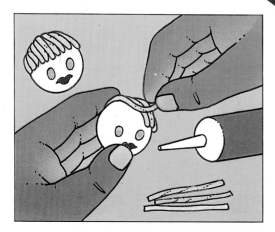

3 Paint a face on a large bead. Cut the gold yarn into pieces about ¾ inch long and glue them to the head for hair.

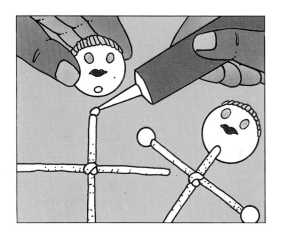

4 For the body, cut a pipe cleaner in half and twist the 2 pieces together, as shown. Dab glue on the ends of the arms and push on the small beads. Dab glue on the neck and push on the head. Put the dress on the body. Pull the yarn ends tightly around the neck and tie them in a bow.

5 Using a pencil, trace the wing pattern on page 57. Turn the tracing paper over and lay it on the back of the gold poster board. Rub firmly over the outline with a pencil. The pattern will appear on the poster board. Cut out one wing. Now lay the shape back on the gold poster board. Draw around it and cut out another wing shape. Glue the shapes together and stick them on the back of the angel. Make 3 angels in this way.

6 Wrap ribbon around the stick and glue the ends in place. Cut the gold cord into 4 lengths. Tie one piece to the ends of the stick, so that the mobile can hang up. Make 3 gold bells by cutting cups from egg cartons and wrapping them in gold foil. Tie each bell onto a length of gold cord, then tie the bells onto the stick. Hang the angels by folding their pipe-cleaner hands over the cord. Tie a ribbon bow at the center of the stick.

YOU WILL NEED
Tracing paper; pencil
Crepe paper
Scissors; all-purpose glue
Gold yarn and needle
Poster paints; paintbrush
White beads (3 large, 6 small)
3 pipe cleaners
Gold poster board
Stick 1 foot long
2 yards of ribbon
1½ yards of gold cord
Egg carton and gold foil

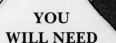

PING-PONG ORNAMENTS

No one would guess these stunning ornaments are made from Ping-Pong balls. You can use paint, glitter, and a few trimmings to make bright and colorful patterns, and ornaments that will make any Christmas tree shine.

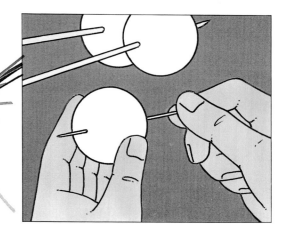

1 Use the darning needle to make a hole through the top and bottom of each Ping-Pong ball. Ask an adult to help you do this. Push a wooden skewer through the holes—this will stop the ball from moving while you are decorating it.

YOU WILL NEED
Darning needle
Ping-Pong balls
Wooden skewers
Poster paint; paintbrush
Braid and trimmings
All-purpose glue
Glitter
Matching thread

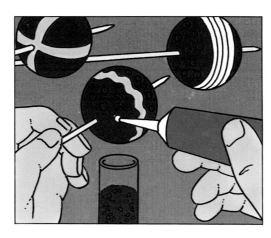

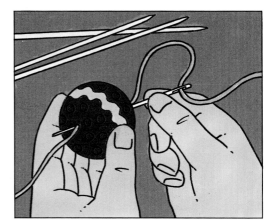

4 When the ornament is decorated, carefully remove the wooden skewer. Thread the needle with fairly thick thread and push it through the holes from bottom to top and then back down again to make a hanging loop. Knot the ends of the thread to finish.

3 Wrap braid around the center of the ball, or from the top to the bottom. Secure the ends with glue. To add glitter, dab glue on the ball and sprinkle with glitter. Leave to dry.

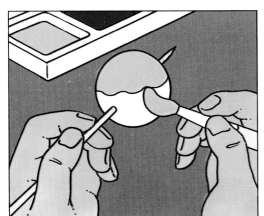

2 Paint the Ping-Pong balls in bright colors. Leave to dry. If the first coat of paint looks a little patchy, add another coat. Leave the paint to dry completely.

3-D GIFT TAGS

Add a special touch to Christmas presents by matching the gift tag to the paper. When making 3-D gift tags, it is best to choose wrapping paper with a repeat pattern that has a clear outline to cut around.

1 Roughly cut around 4 identical motifs from the giftwrap. Glue the motifs to a sheet of paper to make them stiffer.

2 Now carefully cut out 3 of the motifs, following the outline of the shape. From the fourth motif, cut out separate features, such as Santa's face.

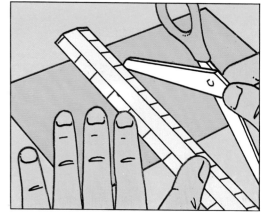

3 Cut a piece of construction paper slightly taller than your chosen motif and at least twice as wide. Score down the center of the paper with a ruler and scissors to make a fold line.

YOU WILL NEED
Giftwrap with
   repeat patterns
Scissors
Glue stick
Plain paper
Colored construction
   paper
Ruler
Double-sided sticky pads
Hole punch
Ribbon

5 Fix the smaller sections from the fourth motif in the appropriate places, using the sticky pads, to create a 3-D effect. Fold the card in half and punch a hole in the top left-hand corner. Thread with ribbon.

4 Turn the construction paper over and glue the first motif to the right-hand side. Position sticky pads all over the motif. Put the second motif on top of the first so that it sticks to the pads. Repeat for the third motif.

MR. FROSTY

Using scraps of felt, make a jolly Mr. Frosty snowman that can be used year after year for a Christmas tree decoration. Simple to carry out yet very effective, this idea can easily be adapted to make Santas.

YOU WILL NEED
Saucer, scissors, and pen
White, orange, and black felt
Needle and thread
White construction paper
Cotton
Large white wooden bead
Red ribbon
All-purpose glue
Black felt-tip pen
Black poster board
Tape

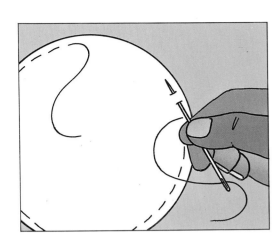

1 Lay a saucer on some white felt, draw around it with a pen, and cut out. Sew around the edge of the circle, as shown. Pull the ends of the thread to draw the felt into a ball shape. Leave a gap in the top and the threads hanging.

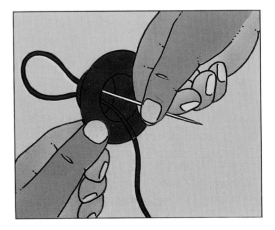

4 For the hat, glue some black felt onto a piece of black poster board. Cut out a circle and make a hole in it large enough to fit over Mr. Frosty's head. This is the brim. Cut a narrow strip of paper and felt. Roll the strip up and push into the brim. Stick in place with tape. Glue a black circle to the top of the hat.

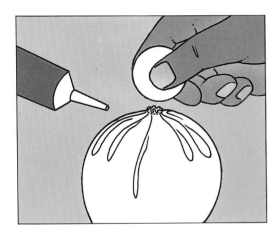

2 Draw a small circle about 1¾ inches in diameter on white construction paper. Cut out and push into the bottom of the white felt ball. Fill the ball with cotton. Pull the ends of the thread tightly and knot securely. Glue the wooden bead to the top of the ball.

3 Cut a piece of ribbon to make a scarf and glue it in place. Use a black felt-tip pen to draw on Mr. Frosty's face, then stick on a piece of orange felt for his nose.

5 Thread a needle with black thread. Push the needle up through the hat and back down again to form a loop. Knot the ends of the thread together inside the hat. Glue the hat to the head.

CHRISTMAS ANGEL

Put this enchanting angel on the top of your Christmas tree as a very special decoration. Her skirt is made from soft pink feathers, but you could give her a white feather skirt if you prefer.

YOU WILL NEED

Tracing paper; pencil
Scissors; masking tape; hole punch
All-purpose glue
2 gold doilies
Poster paints; paintbrush
2-inch white bead
Wooden skewer
Curling gold paper ribbon
1 pipe cleaner
Cotton and ribbon
White and gold poster board
1 yard marabou feather trim

1 Trace the cone and hand patterns on page 58. Turn the tracings over and lay on white poster board. Rub over the outlines with a pencil. The patterns will appear on the card; cut out. Now cut out a second hand shape. Punch holes in the cone for the arms (see pattern). Roll the cones into shape and tape the join.

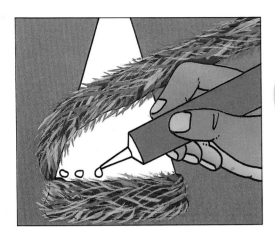

2 Starting at the bottom, wrap the feather trim around the cone. Use small dabs of glue to hold it in place. To make the collar, cut a section from one of the doilies and glue it around the top of the cone.

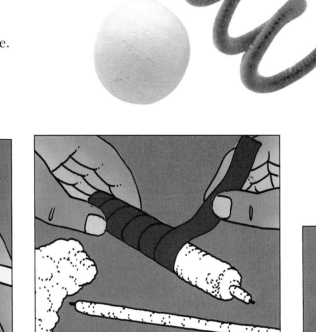

3 Paint a face on the bead. Dribble some glue into the hole in the bead and push in the skewer. Glue lengths of curling ribbon onto the bead for hair.

4 To make the arms, cut a pipe cleaner into two 3-inch lengths. Glue cotton around each one. Leave ¼ inch at each end uncovered. Wrap ribbon over the cotton and keep in place with a dab of glue. Glue on the white poster-board hands.

5 Push the arms into the holes in the cone. Push the head into the cone. From the gold poster board, cut a small rectangle for the book and a circle for the halo. Fold the book in half and glue the hands to each side of it. Fold the second doily in half and glue to the angel for wings. Glue the halo onto the head.

STENCILED GLITTER CARDS

This form of stenciling uses glitter and glue to make the shapes instead of paint. The stencil is cut from firm paper and can be used again and again to print lots of cards or gift tags.

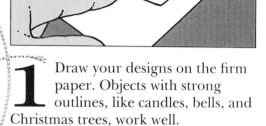

1 Draw your designs on the firm paper. Objects with strong outlines, like candles, bells, and Christmas trees, work well.

YOU WILL NEED
Pencil and ruler
Firm paper for stencil
Scissors
Colored construction paper
Glue stick
Glitter in different colors
Hole punch
Ribbon

30

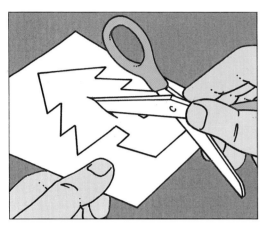

2 Push the scissor point into the center of your design, as shown. Carefully cut out the shape to make a "window" in the paper. This is the stencil.

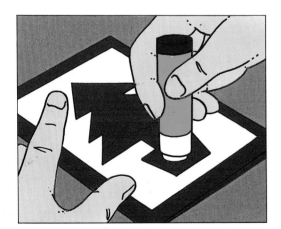

3 Cut the construction paper into a rectangle. Place the stencil on top of the card and, holding it firmly in place, apply the glue to the card through the cut-out shape.

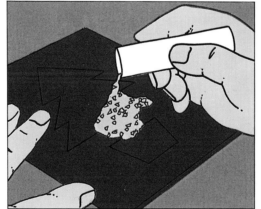

4 When all the cut-out area has been completely covered with glue, carefully lift off the stencil. While the glue is still wet, sprinkle the glitter on it. Leave to dry.

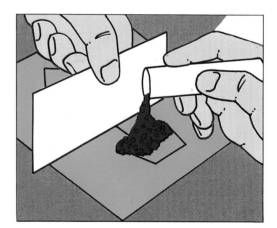

5 To make the glitter stripes, hold the straight edge of a spare piece of construction paper or cardboard over some of the glued surface, then shake on the glitter. Move the card and apply another color of glitter. Do this until the shape is covered. To finish, punch a hole through one corner of the card and thread some ribbon through it.

SAFETY TIP: *Make sure an adult helps you when using sharp scissors.*

MINI CARD WREATHS

Decorate your Christmas tree this year with these little wreaths, made from poster board, ribbons, and glittery sequins. The designs shown here are just a guide. You could also try decorating the wreaths with dried flowers or holly leaves and berries.

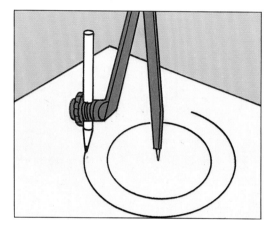

1 Using the compass, draw a circle about 2½ inches in diameter on the poster board. Leaving the point of the compass in the same position, draw a second circle about 1½ inches larger than the first. Carefully cut out the wreath.

2 Dab some glue on the end of a length of ribbon and press it to the back of the wreath. When the glue has dried, twist the ribbon around and around the wreath so that all the board is covered. Glue the end of the ribbon to the back of the wreath.

3 Repeat with another trim, like sequin strips, this time forming it in much bigger loops. You may want to glue individual sequins on as well. Make a small bow from ribbon of another color and glue it to the top of the wreath.

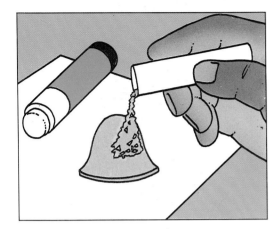

4 Cut out a bell shape from the poster board and lay it on a sheet of scrap paper. Cover the bell with glue and, while it is still wet, sprinkle glitter on top. Leave it to dry.

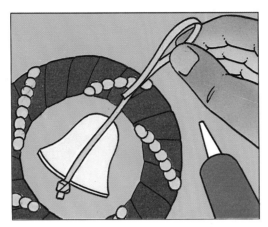

5 Cut a piece of cord about 6 inches long and tie a knot at one end. Glue the end of the cord to the back of the bell. Position the bell in the center of the wreath, taking the cord up at the back. Fold the cord back down into a loop and glue it behind the wreath.

YOU WILL NEED
Compass and pencil
Poster board
Scissors
All-purpose glue
Ribbons, cords,
   and sequins
Scraps of
   poster board
Glitter

RIBBON ROSETTES

These ribbon rosettes are very quick and easy to make, yet they give a really stylish finish to your Christmas presents. Try tying your presents with shiny metallic ribbon and making a matching rosette for the top.

YOU WILL NEED
Scissors
Shiny giftwrap ribbon
Ruler
Double-sided tape

1 Cut 8 lengths of ribbon 8 inches long. Cut a small piece of ribbon 2 inches long, for the central loop.

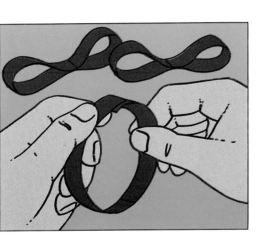

4 To make a two-color bow, cut 4 pieces each of 2 differently colored ribbons. Make 8 bow loops as in Step 2. Crisscross the loops, using first one color, then another, before finishing with a small center loop.

3 Tape the loops together by placing each diagonally on top of the one below, to form a crisscross pattern. To finish, tape the ends of the short piece of ribbon together to form a tiny loop. Tape this neatly in the center of the rosette.

2 Overlap the ends of each of the long lengths of ribbon and stick together with double-sided tape to form a loop. Join each loop in the middle, using tape on the inside of the loop, as shown.

SANTA PUPPET

Make this smiling Santa puppet to give away as a Christmas present or to keep for yourself. You can also try drawing your own patterns to create a whole family of puppet characters.

1 Using a pencil, trace the patterns on page 59. You will need 3 patterns to make the Santa. Trace the body pattern around the solid line, the face pattern around the dotted line, and the beard around the broken line. Cut out the 3 patterns. Pin the body pattern onto red felt and cut out 2 shapes.

2 Pin the face pattern onto pink felt and cut out. Glue the face to one puppet shape. Sew on the red bead nose. Stitch the 2 body shapes together, leaving the bottom of the puppet open.

YOU WILL NEED
Tracing paper and pencil
Scissors
Pins
Red, pink, and black felt
Fabric glue
Red thread and needle
1 red bead
White fur fabric

3 Pin the beard pattern to the back of the fur fabric. Cut out the beard and carefully cut out the mouth as marked. Glue the beard under Santa's nose.

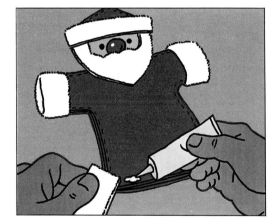

4 Cut out strips of fur fabric to fit around the bottom of the puppet, around each arm, and around the head. Glue the strips in place. Cut out 2 black felt eyes and glue in position on the face. Cut out a fur-fabric hat pompom and glue to the top of the hat.

STARS AND BELLS

These bright and shiny stars and bells are easy to make and will look very pretty hanging from your Christmas tree. You can also make a colorful garland by stringing the decorations onto ribbon.

YOU WILL NEED
Tracing paper and pencil
Scissors
Shiny cardboard
Hole punch
Star stickers
Shiny giftwrap ribbon

1 Using a pencil, trace the patterns on page 60. Cut out the patterns and hold in position on the back of the shiny cardboard. Draw around the patterns and cut out the shapes.

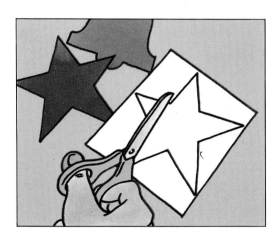

2 To make more stars and bells, lay the shapes you have just cut out on cardboard and draw around them. Cut out as many shapes as you like.

3 Punch a hole in your decorations so you will be able to hang them up. Decorate them with gold and silver stars.

4 Thread ribbon through the holes you have made. To make a garland, thread lots of stars and bells onto ribbon.

REINDEER HAT

Add to the Christmas spirit with this jolly reindeer party hat. Make your hat as glamorous as you can by adding lots of shiny ribbon, glitter, and beads.

YOU WILL NEED
Scissors
Green and beige poster board
All-purpose glue
Giftwrap ribbon
Strings of beads
Tracing paper and pencil
Black felt-tip pen
Wooden bead
Red glitter
3 yellow pipe cleaners
2 bells

1 Cut a strip of green poster board 3¼ inches wide and long enough to go around your head, with overlap. Overlap the ends and glue together. Glue giftwrap ribbon and beads in loops around the hat.

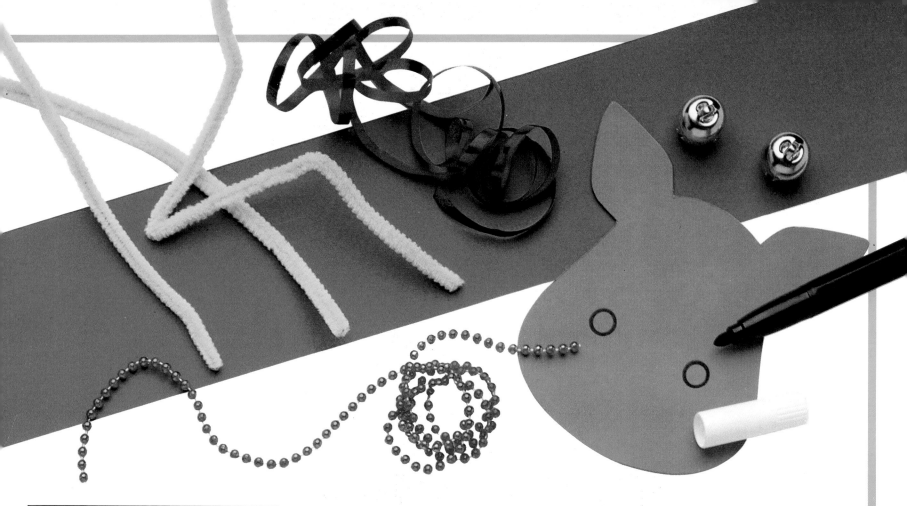

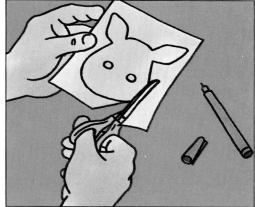

2 Using a pencil, trace the reindeer face on page 61. Turn the tracing paper over and lay it on the beige poster board. Rub firmly over the outline with a pencil. The image will appear on the poster board. Cut out the face. Draw the eyes with a felt-tip pen.

3 Cover the wooden bead with glue and sprinkle it with glitter. Leave to dry and then glue it to the reindeer's face. To make the antlers, bend the pipe cleaners in half and glue them behind the head.

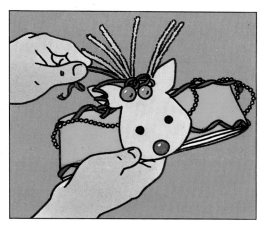

4 Glue the reindeer face to the green poster-board strip. Tie the bells onto some ribbon and tie these around the antlers so that they rest between the reindeer's ears. Bend the pipe cleaners over slightly to give the antlers some shape.

ROYAL CROWN

If you have to dress up for a Christmas costume party, go as one of the Three Kings, wearing this fabulous crown. Decorate it with colored foil to look like jewels.

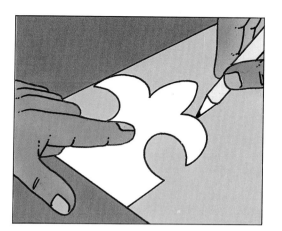

1 Using a pencil, trace the pattern on page 61. Turn the tracing paper over and lay it on a piece of scrap cardboard. Rub firmly over the outline with a pencil. The image will appear on the cardboard. Cut out the pattern. This is one section of the crown. Put the pattern on the gold cardboard so that the straight edges match up. Draw around the shape.

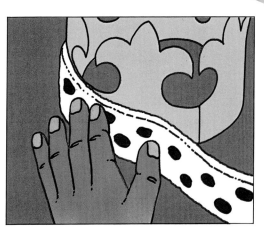

2 Move the pattern along and position it against the shape you have just drawn, as shown. Make sure the short sides match. Draw around the shape again. Repeat this until you have drawn around the pattern 5 times.

3 Carefully cut out the crown shape. Paint black dashes on the wadding and leave it to dry. Curve the crown into shape, overlapping the edges. Tape the join on the inside. Glue the wadding to the lower edge of the crown, butting the edges together.

4 Cut squares from the colored foil and glue them onto the crown.

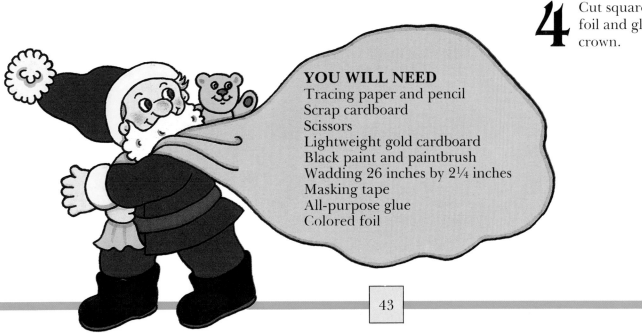

YOU WILL NEED
Tracing paper and pencil
Scrap cardboard
Scissors
Lightweight gold cardboard
Black paint and paintbrush
Wadding 26 inches by 2¼ inches
Masking tape
All-purpose glue
Colored foil

TOTE BAGS

Paper tote bags are much easier to make than they look and are great for wrapping awkwardly shaped Christmas presents. You can line Christmas giftwrap with plain paper to make sturdy tote bags in a variety of sizes. Use white paper for the lining, or a color to match the giftwrap.

1 To make the lining, cut a piece of plain paper large enough to wrap around 2 or 3 books, with at least 2 inches extra at the top and bottom.

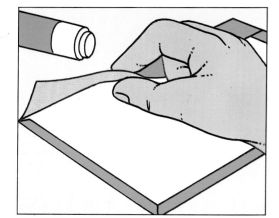

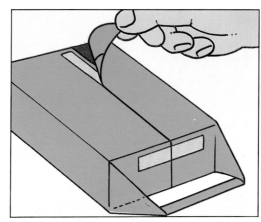

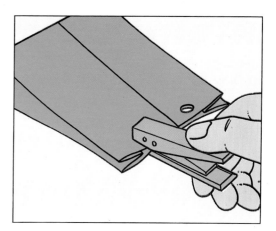

2 Cut a piece of giftwrap ½ inch larger all around than the plain paper. Glue the plain paper to the wrong side of the giftwrap. Fold in the edges of the giftwrap and glue them down. Fold the top edge down again by about 2 inches.

3 Wrap the lined giftwrap around the books. Join the long edges together, using double-sided tape. Make the base of the bag by folding in the bottom edges as you would when wrapping a present in the usual way. Seal the base with double-sided tape.

4 Carefully slide the books out of the bag. Pinch the sides of the bag together to form a crease down the center of each side. Hold the top edges together and punch 2 holes through both thicknesses of giftwrap.

YOU WILL NEED
Scissors
1 large sheet of plain paper
Books to act as mold
Christmas giftwrap
Glue stick
Double-sided tape
Hole punch
Giftwrap ribbon

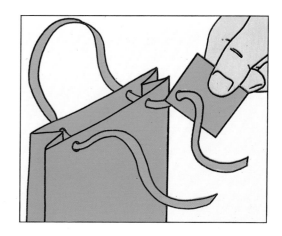

5 Cut a small square of giftwrap for a tag. Glue a square of plain paper to the back. Punch a hole in one corner of the tag and thread it onto the ribbon. Thread the ribbon through the holes in the bag to make handles. Tie the ends together.

PYRAMID GIFT BAGS

These pyramid-shaped gift bags are a great idea for making gifts look extra special at Christmas. Make small bags to hang on the Christmas tree or larger ones to give as presents. Fill them to the top with candy or tiny gifts.

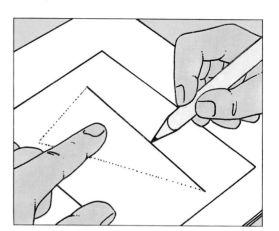

1 Using a pencil, trace either the large or the small triangle pattern on page 62. Turn the tracing over and lay it on a piece of cardboard. Rub firmly over the outline with a pencil. The pattern will appear on the cardboard. Cut out the shape.

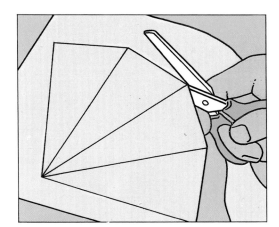

2 Lay the pattern on the thin poster board and draw around it 4 times, as shown. Keep the point in the same place each time and move the pattern along so that the long sides are edge-to-edge. Cut out the whole shape in one complete piece.

YOU WILL NEED
Tracing paper and pencil
Scrap cardboard
Scissors
Thin poster board
Glue stick
Giftwrap
Hole punch
Ribbon or golden chain

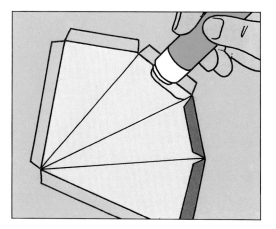

3 Coat the shape with glue and stick it to the wrong side of a sheet of giftwrap. Cut around the shape, leaving an extra 1 inch of giftwrap all around. Fold this over and glue to the poster board.

4 Fold the bag shape along 3 sides, as shown. Glue 2 sections together to make a pyramid shape. Leave to dry.

5 Punch a hole in the center of each section at the top. Thread ribbon or a golden chain through the holes to make handles. Tie the ends together.

SALT-DOUGH CANDLE HOLDERS

These sparkling star candle holders are made from salt dough—just flour, salt, and water—painted and covered in glitter. Despite the fact that they sound edible, they are not!

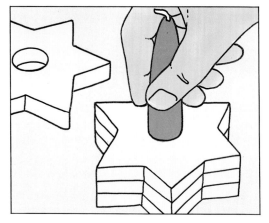

1 Put the flour and salt in the bowl and, with the wooden spoon, mix in the water a little at a time until the mixture forms a ball of dough. Sprinkle some extra flour on your work surface and put the dough in the center. Roll out the dough until it is about ½ inch thick.

2 Preheat the oven to 325° F. Using a pencil, trace one of the large star patterns on page 63. Turn the tracing over and lay it on a piece of poster board. Rub firmly over the outline with a pencil. The pattern will appear on the poster board. Cut out the shape. Lay the pattern on the dough and cut around it. Cut out 3 stars of the same size for each candle holder.

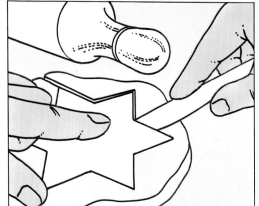

3 Press the base of your candle into 2 of the stars, then cut this circle away. Carefully place the 2 stars with the holes in them on the uncut star, lining up the points. Lift the star onto the baking sheet. Check that the candle still fits. If you prefer, make a round candle holder and decorate it with small star shapes. Trace the small star from the pattern on page 63.

YOU WILL NEED
2 cups all-purpose flour
1 cup salt
Mixing bowl and wooden spoon
1 cup water
Rolling pin and blunt knife
Tracing paper and pencil
Scrap poster board
Baking sheet and oven mitts
Candles
Poster paints and paintbrush
All-purpose glue
Glitter

SAFETY TIP: *Make sure an adult helps you when using the oven.*

4 Bake the candle holders for about 30 minutes. Using oven mitts, remove them from the oven. Once they are cooled, put the holders on newspaper and paint them with poster paints.

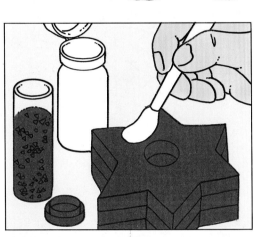

5 When the paint has dried, apply glue all over the holder and sprinkle with glitter. Do not move the holder until the glue has dried.

GINGERBREAD MEN

Delicious and fun to eat, these gingerbread men can also be hung on the Christmas tree as decorations. If you do hang them up, remember that you should eat them within a couple of days, or they will become dirty and stale.

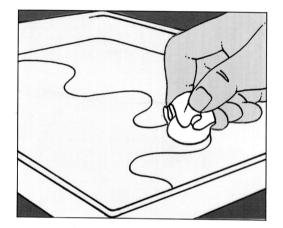

1 Preheat the oven to 350° F. Grease a baking sheet with a little butter. Sift the dry ingredients in a mixing bowl.

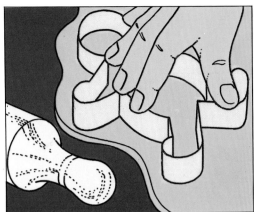

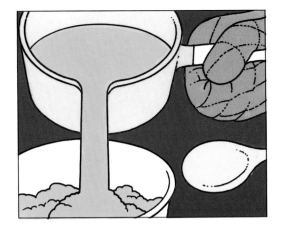

2 Put the butter, molasses, and sugar in a saucepan and heat gently until they have melted. Pour the melted mixture into the bowl of dry ingredients and add the beaten egg. Mix all the ingredients together to form a ball of dough.

3 Sprinkle a little flour on your work surface and, using a rolling pin, roll out the dough until it is about ⅛ inch thick. Cut out the cookies with a gingerbread man cutter. Transfer the shapes onto the baking sheet.

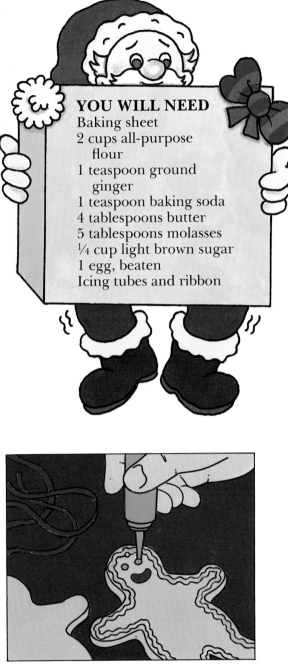

YOU WILL NEED
Baking sheet
2 cups all-purpose
   flour
1 teaspoon ground
   ginger
1 teaspoon baking soda
4 tablespoons butter
5 tablespoons molasses
¼ cup light brown sugar
1 egg, beaten
Icing tubes and ribbon

4 Bake the gingerbread men for about 20 minutes, until they are brown around the edges. Wearing oven mitts, remove the baking sheet from the oven. While the cookies are still warm, make a hole in the top of the head, using the tip of a skewer.

5 When the gingerbread men have cooled, use icing tubes to decorate them. Tie a ribbon through the hole in the top.

SAFETY TIP: *Make sure an adult helps you when using the oven.*

FESTIVE FUDGE

Vanilla fudge is fun to make, and quite simple. Pack it in glittery cellophane or small boxes to make a delicious Christmas present.

YOU WILL NEED
8-by-8-inch baking pan
Wax paper
2 cups sugar
½ cup butter
15-ounce can condensed milk
Few drops of vanilla extract
Large, heavy-based saucepan
Wooden spoon
Knife

1 Line the pan with the wax paper before you start to cook. Set aside.

2 Put the sugar, butter, condensed milk, and vanilla in a large, heavy-based saucepan. Heat gently, stirring all the time with a wooden spoon, until the sugar has dissolved and the butter has melted.

3 Bring the mixture to a boil. Boil for 10 to 15 minutes, stirring continuously, until the mixture has thickened and turned a golden-brown color. Turn off the heat.

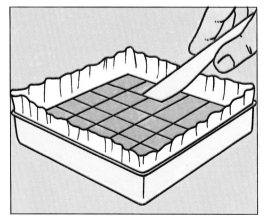

4 Pour the mixture into the pan and smooth flat. Using a knife, lightly mark squares on the top of the fudge. Leave to cool completely before removing from the pan and cutting the fudge into squares.

SAFETY TIP: *Make sure an adult helps you when using the oven.*

PATTERNS

Some of the projects in this book are based on the patterns given on the following pages. To find out how to copy a pattern, follow the step-by-step instructions given for each project.

   You may want to make a pattern that you can keep to use again. To do this, trace over the outline of the pattern on tracing paper with a pencil. Turn your tracing over and lay it on a piece of cardboard or poster board. Rub firmly over the outline with a pencil. The image will appear on the cardboard or poster board. Cut out the shape. If you keep this pattern in a safe place, you can use it time and time again.

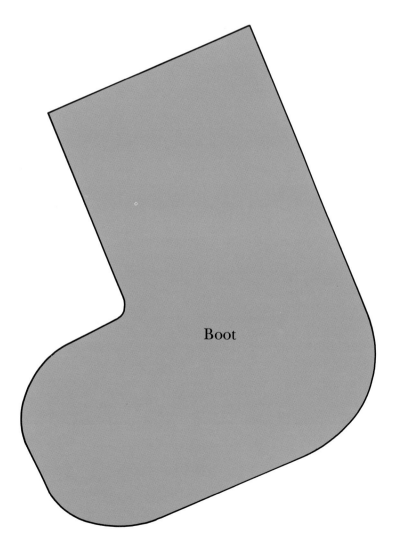

Boot

Candle

FELT TREE ORNAMENTS
Page **8**

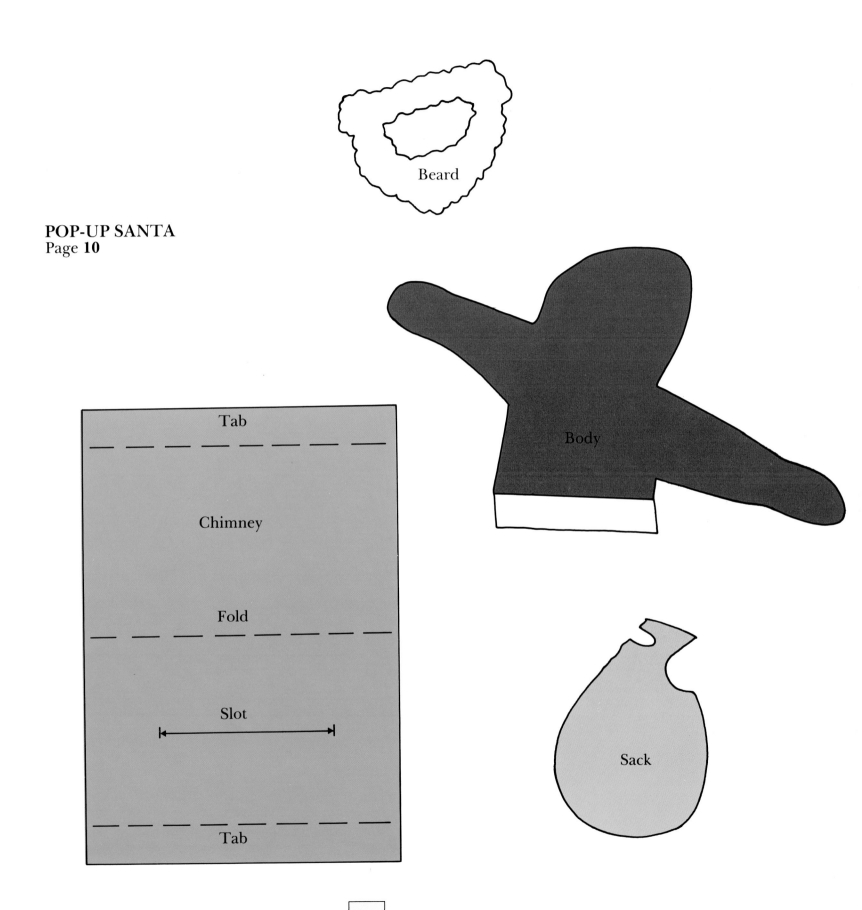

Beard

POP-UP SANTA
Page **10**

Tab

Chimney

Fold

Slot

Tab

Body

Sack

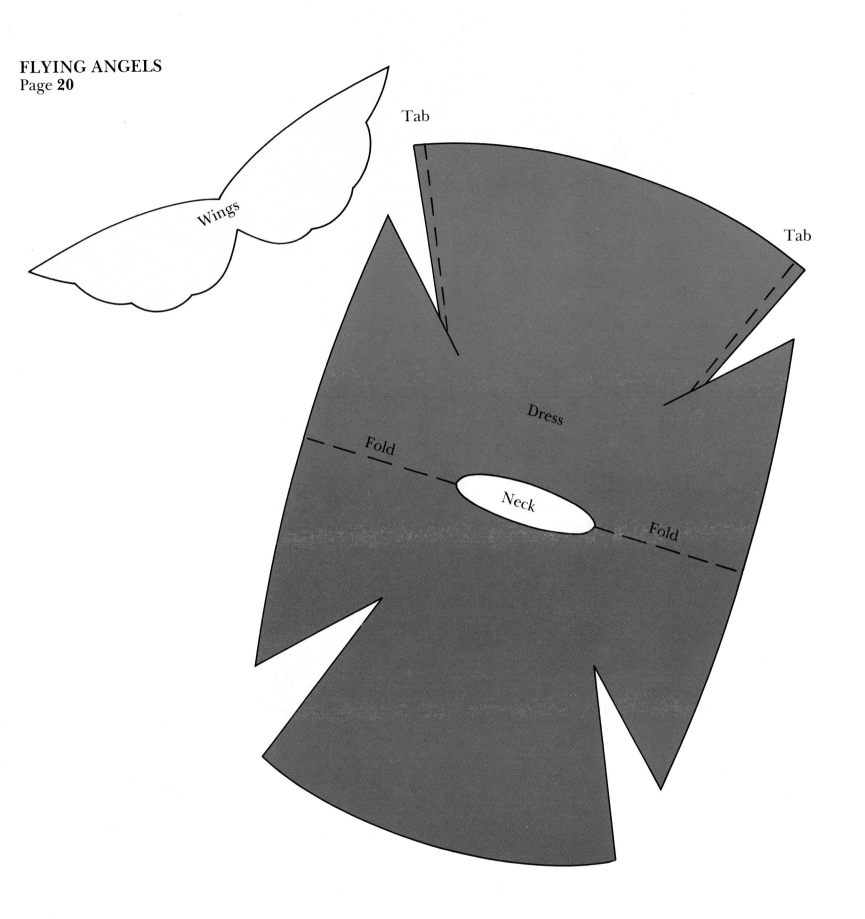

Tab

Tab

Wings

Dress

Fold

Neck

Fold

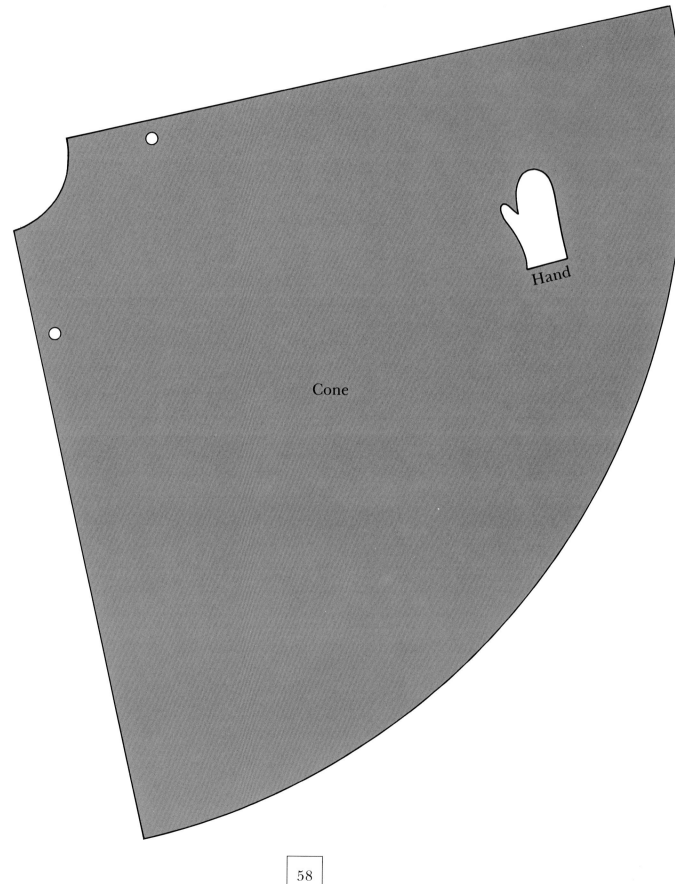

Hand

Cone

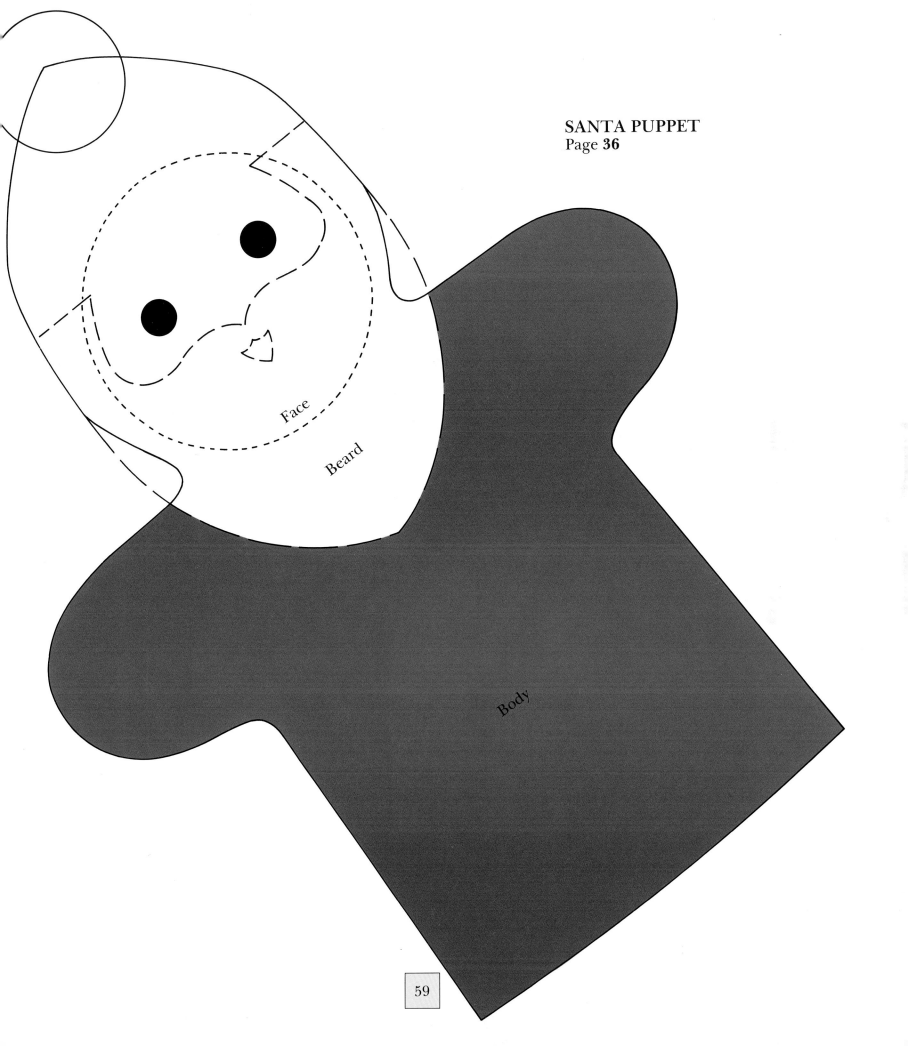

SANTA PUPPET
Page **36**

Face

Beard

Body

59

STARS AND BELLS
Page **38**

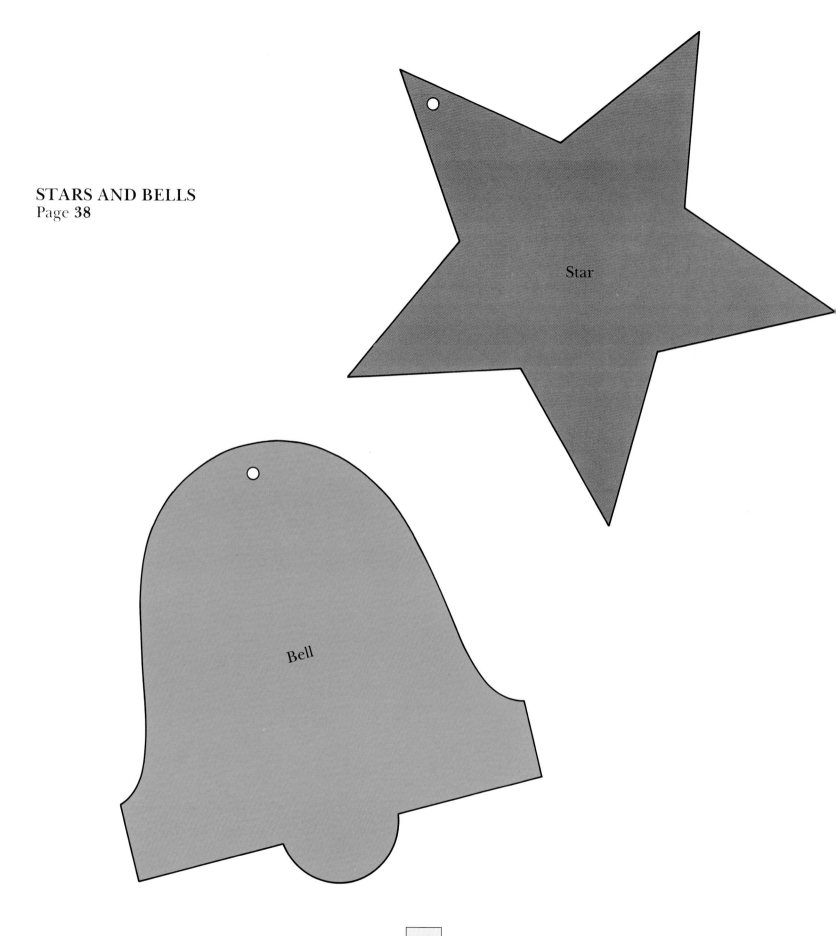

Star

Bell

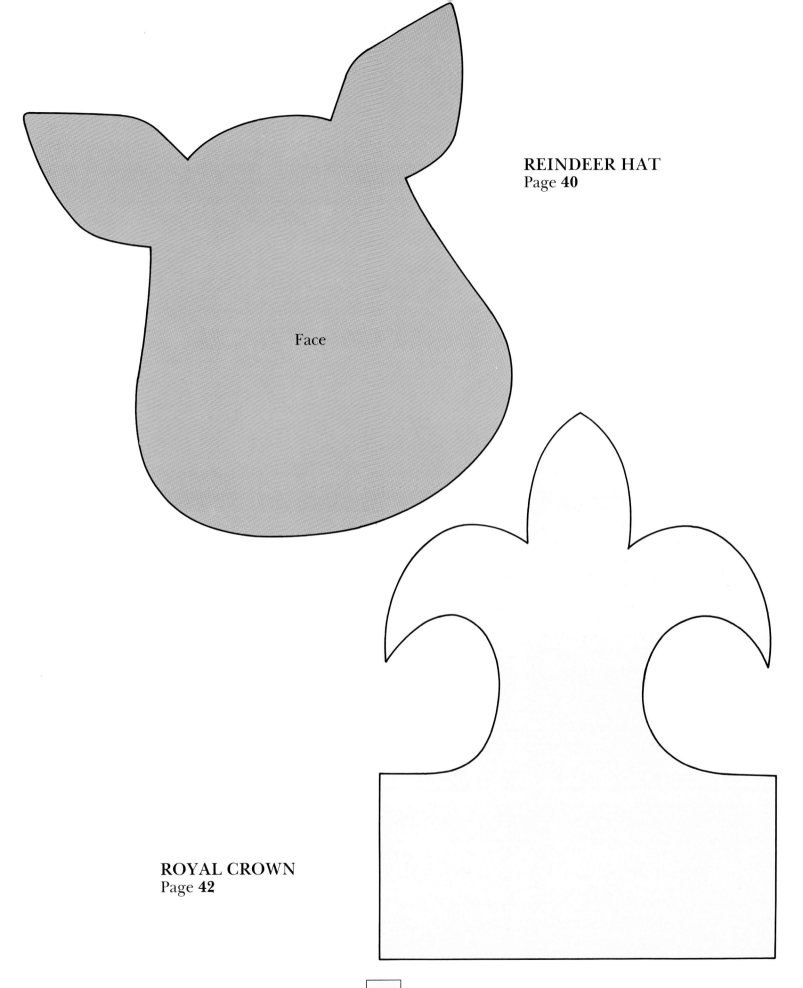

REINDEER HAT
Page **40**

Face

ROYAL CROWN
Page **42**

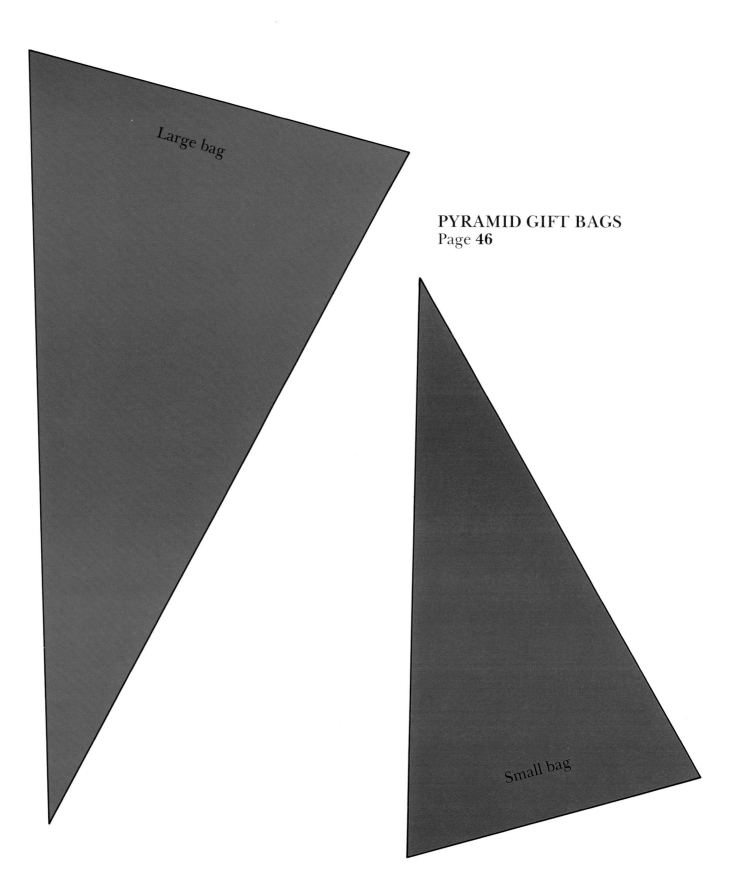

Large bag

PYRAMID GIFT BAGS
Page **46**

Small bag

INDEX

ACKNOWLEDGMENT
The publishers would like to thank Hallmark Cards Ltd, Henley-on-Thames, Oxon, for their help in compiling this book.